vasilisa
THe BeaUTIFUL

vasilisa
THE BEAUTIFUL

TRANSLATED FROM THE RUSSIAN
BY THOMAS P. WHITNEY ✕✕✕✕✕
ILLUSTRATED BY NONNY HOGROGIAN

THE MACMILLAN COMPANY · COLLIER-MACMILLAN LTD., LONDON

FOR LITTLE JULIE

ONCE UPON A TIME in a distant kingdom there lived a
merchant. In twelve years of marriage he and his wife had had
only one daughter, whom they named Vasilisa the Beautiful.
Vasilisa was eight years old when her mother became ill and
lay dying. She called the girl to her bedside, took a doll from
beneath the bedcover, and gave it to her.

"Listen carefully, dear Vasilisa," she said. "Remember my
words and do as I say. I leave you my blessing and this little
doll. Keep her with you always and never show her to anyone.
Should you be in trouble give her something to eat and ask her
advice. When she has eaten, she will tell you what to do."

The mother kissed Vasilisa and died.

The merchant observed the accepted period of mourning, and then began to think about marrying again. He was a good man and there were many brides to choose from. But of them all, a certain widow pleased him the most. She was suitable in every way and had two daughters about Vasilisa's age. And as she seemed to be a good housekeeper and mother, she was the one the merchant married. But the merchant had been deceived, for as it turned out his new wife was not a good mother to Vasilisa.

Vasilisa was the most beautiful girl in the village, and her stepmother and stepsisters were jealous of her. They made her do all the heavy chores in and around the house hoping that she would grow scrawny from overwork and that her skin would be spoiled by the wind and the sun. They tried in every way to make her life as miserable as possible.

Vasilisa, however, suffered everything without a murmur, each day growing plumper and prettier while the stepmother and her two daughters became thinner and uglier out of meanness. It did not help them to sit around lazily with their hands folded, doing nothing as if they were noblewomen.

The truth was that the little doll was helping Vasilisa.

How else could she have done all the work! Indeed Vasilisa often would not eat enough herself and would save the tastiest morsels on her plate for her doll. At night when everyone was asleep, she would lock herself in the storeroom where she was made to live. Then she would set the food before the doll and say:

"Here you are, my little doll! Eat and hear what misfortune has befallen me. In my own father's house, there's nothing but unhappiness for me. My evil stepmother wants to drive me into the grave. What am I to do? Please tell me?"

When the doll had eaten she told Vasilisa what she was to do and comforted her in her grief. By morning the doll had done all of Vasilisa's work so that the girl could just sit in a shady spot, or pick flowers. All the seedbeds had been weeded, water brought from the well and the stove started. The doll had also found an herb for Vasilisa that protected her from the sun. With the doll's help everything was taken care of.

Several years passed and Vasilisa reached marriageable age. All the young men of the village courted her and wanted her as a bride, but not one of them even so much as looked at her stepsisters. The stepmother, who was now more envious than ever, drove all Vasilisa's suitors away with the same words: "I will not have the youngest engaged before her elder sisters have found husbands."

After showing Vasilisa's suitors the door, she would fly into a rage and beat her.

It happened that the merchant's business took him away from home for a long period. During his absence the stepmother moved with her two daughters and Vasilisa to a house on the outskirts of a deep forest. In the middle of the forest in an open clearing stood a hut that belonged to Baba Yaga. She allowed no one into her house or yard, and, when humans strayed into her path, she devoured them as if they were chickens. From time to time the stepmother would find errands for Vasilisa in the forest, but Vasilisa always returned home safely. The doll showed her the way and kept her a safe distance from Baba Yaga's hut.

Autumn came. One evening the stepmother gave all three daughters work to do. One was to weave lace, the other was to knit stockings, and Vasilisa was to spin. After giving each one instructions, the stepmother snuffed all the candles but one for the girls to work by and went off to bed. The girls worked until the candle began to flicker. One of Vasilisa's stepsisters got up to trim the wick, but following her mother's instructions, she extinguished it instead, as if by accident.

"What are we to do now?" said the stepsisters. "There's not a light to be had in the entire house and we haven't finished our work. We must get a light from Baba Yaga!"

The stepsister who was weaving lace said, "My pins give me enough light and so I have no need to go."

"I don't have to go either," said the stepsister who was knitting stockings. "I get enough light from my needles."

Both turned to Vasilisa and cried: "You are the one who must fetch a light. Go to Baba Yaga!" And with that they pushed her out of the house.

Vasilisa had again been made to sleep in the storeroom and there she went. She put the food she had prepared for her doll before her and said:

"Here you are, little doll! Eat and hear what misfortune has befallen me. I must fetch a light from Baba Yaga and surely she will eat me up!"

The doll ate. Her eyes gleamed like two candles.

"Don't be afraid, Vasilisa!" she said. "Go where they send you, but take me along. You will be safe as long as I am with you."

Vasilisa gathered up her things and put the little doll in her pocket. She crossed herself and went off into the deep forest. She walked and walked all night long. Suddenly a white horseman dashed past her. Everything about him was white—his clothes, the horse beneath him, even the horse's saddle, bridle and reins were white. And immediately it began to grow light.

Vasilisa walked on, and another horseman dashed by. This one was red, was dressed in red and rode a red horse. And immediately the sun began to rise.

Vasilisa walked the entire day, and it was not until evening that she reached the clearing where Baba Yaga's hut stood. It was surrounded by a fence made of human bones topped by human skulls. Leg bones made up the gateposts, skeletons' hands served as bolts, and instead of a lock there was a mouth with sharp teeth. Vasilisa grew faint with fear and stood rooted to the spot. Suddenly a third horseman rode up. He was black, his clothes were black and he was mounted on a black horse. He rode right up to Baba Yaga's gates—and disappeared as if he had fallen through the earth. And immediately night fell. But the darkness did not last long. The skulls' eyes lit up, and it became as bright in the clearing as if it were noon. Vasilisa trembled with fear, but not knowing where to flee she stayed where she was.

Soon a terrible noise came from the forest. The trees creaked and the dry leaves crackled. Out of the woods came Baba Yaga riding in a mortar, pushing her way along with a pestle and sweeping the tracks it left behind with a broom. She rode up to the gates, stopped, sniffed and cried out:

"Foo, foo, I smell a Russian! Who is here?"

Vasilisa went fearfully up to the old woman and, bowing low, said, "It is I, Granny! My stepsisters sent me to you to get a light."

"Very good," said Baba Yaga. "I know them well. From now on you will live here and work for me. If you do what I tell you I will give you a light, and if you don't I will eat you up!" Turning to the gates, she cried out: "Hey there, my strong bolts, unlock! My broad gates, open wide!"

The gates opened and Baba Yaga entered, whistling. Vasilisa followed behind her and the gates closed.

Once inside the hut Baba Yaga sprawled out and said to Vasilisa, "Serve me what you find in the oven. I want to eat."

Vasilisa went out, lit a candle from a skull on the fence and returned to the hut. She took the food out of the oven and served it to Baba Yaga. There was enough for ten people. From the cellar Vasilisa brought up kvas and mead, beer and wine. The old woman ate and drank everything. She left Vasilisa only a bit of cabbage soup, a crust of bread and one little piece of meat.

Then Baba Yaga got ready for bed and said to Vasilisa, "After I leave tomorrow you are to clean up the yard, sweep the house, make my dinner, wash my linens, and in addition you must go to the grain bin, take six bushels of wheat and clean them of weed seeds. Now see to it you do everything I've told you to. Otherwise I will eat you up!"

After giving Vasilisa these instructions Baba Yaga fell asleep and began to snore. Vasilisa put the food given her by the old woman in front of the doll, burst into tears and said:

"Here you are, little doll! Eat and hear what misfortune has befallen me. Baba Yaga has given me very hard work to do and she will eat me up if I don't get it all done. Please help me!"

"Don't be afraid, Vasilisa!" the doll replied. "Get yourself something to eat, say your prayers, and lie down to sleep. Things always look brighter in the morning."

Vasilisa awoke very early but Baba Yaga was already up and looking out of the window. The eyes of the skulls were growing dim. The white horseman dashed past—and it grew light. Baba Yaga went into her yard and whistled and her pestle, mortar and broom appeared before her. Then the red horseman dashed past and the sun rose. Baba Yaga climbed into the mortar and rode out of the yard, pushing her way along with the pestle and covering her tracks with her broom. Vasilisa was left all alone. She went through Baba Yaga's house and was astonished to see how much of everything there was. She hesitated a moment not knowing where to begin, but as she looked around she saw that everything had been done. The little doll was already separating the last bits of weed seed from the wheat.

"You have saved me again!" Vasilisa said to the doll.

"The only thing still to be done is to make dinner," replied the doll, climbing back into Vasilisa's pocket. "God bless you, go and cook it and then take a good rest."

By evening Vasilisa had set the table and was waiting for Baba Yaga. Twilight began to fall and the black horseman dashed past. Then and there it grew dark and the skulls' eyes began to gleam. The trees creaked and the leaves crackled and Baba Yaga approached. Vasilisa went out to meet her.

"Have you done everything?" asked Baba Yaga.

"Look and see for yourself, if you please, Granny," Vasilisa replied.

Baba Yaga inspected all and because there was nothing to which she could object fell into a bad mood.

"Well all right!" she said grudgingly. Then she cried out: "My faithful servants, my loyal friends, grind my grain."

Three pairs of hands appeared, took the grain and carried it out of sight. Baba Yaga ate her meal, began to get ready for bed, and once more gave Vasilisa instructions.

"Tomorrow you are to do the same things as you did today. But in addition you must take the poppy seeds from the grain bin and clean each one separately, for someone spiteful has mixed dirt with them."

After giving her orders the old woman turned her face to the wall and began to snore. Vasilisa again fed her doll. The doll ate and just as she had the night before said to Vasilisa:

"Say your prayers and lie down to sleep. The morning is brighter than the evening. Everything will be done, Vasilisa."

When morning came Baba Yaga once again rode out of the yard in her mortar, and Vasilisa and the doll immediately set about their work. The old woman returned at night, inspected everything and cried out: "My faithful servants, loyal friends, press the poppy seed into oil."

Three pairs of hands appeared, got the poppy seed and took it out of sight. Baba Yaga began to eat her dinner. She sat there eating while Vasilisa stood silently by.

"Why don't you talk to me?" asked Baba Yaga. "You stand there as if you were dumb."

"I don't dare," answered Vasilisa, "but if I may I'd like to ask you some questions."

"Go ahead and ask, but remember that the answers to questions don't always lead to a good end. If you know too much, you'll grow old quickly."

"I only wanted to ask you, Granny, about some things that I saw on my way to your house. I saw a white horseman, dressed all in white on a white horse. Who was he?"

"That was my day so clear," Baba Yaga replied.

"And then another horseman passed me—a red horseman, dressed in red on a red horse. Who was he?"

"That was my sun so red!" replied Baba Yaga.

"And what about the black horseman who passed me just as I came up to your gates, Granny?"

"That was my night so dark! All three are my faithful servants!"

Vasilisa remembered the three pairs of hands but was silent.

"Why don't you ask me anything more?" inquired Baba Yaga.

"If I do, Granny, maybe what you said will happen to me—you said that if one knows too much one grows old quickly!"

"It's a good thing," said Baba Yaga, "that you asked only about what you saw outside my courtyard and not inside it! I don't like my affairs talked about, and I eat up anyone who gets too curious! And now I want to ask you a question. How did you manage to do all the work I gave you?"

"My mother's blessing helped me," Vasilisa replied.

"So that's it!" exclaimed Baba Yaga. "Then get out of here! I don't want anyone around me who is blessed."

She dragged Vasilisa out of the house and pushed her outside the gates. Then she removed a skull with burning eyes from the fence, stuck it on a stick and gave it to Vasilisa, saying, "Here's a light for your stepsisters. Take it with you. That's what they sent you for, isn't it?"

Vasilisa started for home, her path illumined by the skull's light, which went out each morning and relit itself each night. At long last, by the evening of the following day, she arrived home. When she reached the gates she was about to throw away the skull. "Now I am home," she thought to herself, "and by this time they have surely got their own light."

But suddenly she heard a hollow voice from within the skull: "Do not throw me away. Take me to your stepmother!"

She looked into the house and, seeing no light in any of the windows, decided to do as the voice said. She was greeted cordially by her stepmother and stepsisters, who told her that there had been no light at all in the house since she had gone. They had been unable to strike one themselves, and whatever light they had got elsewhere had gone out as soon as it was brought inside.

"Perhaps your light will last," the stepmother said.

No sooner had she spoken these words than the skull began to cast burning rays on her and her daughters! They tried to hide—but the eyes pursued them everywhere until all that was left of them was ashes. Only Vasilisa remained unharmed.

The next morning Vasilisa buried the skull in the earth, locked up the house and went off to the city. There she found a place to live with an old woman who had no family of her own. Vasilisa stayed with her, waiting for her father to return.

One day she said to the old woman, "I'm very bored sitting here with no work, Granny! Would you buy me some of the best quality hemp you can get. Then at least I can spin!"

The old woman bought good hemp, and Vasilisa went busily to work. The yarn she spun came out as smooth and as fine as a hair. She worked up a large amount ready for weaving into linen. But there was no loom to be found with a comb fine enough for Vasilisa's yarn, and no one was willing to undertake such a delicate job. So Vasilisa asked her doll to help her, and the doll said:

"Go get me an old comb, an old shuttle and a horse's mane. I will weave this yarn myself."

Vasilisa got everything the doll needed and then lay down to sleep. The doll built a loom in one night. By the end of the winter the cloth had been woven and it was so fine that it could be pulled through the eye of a needle. In the spring the cloth was bleached and Vasilisa said to the old woman:

"Please go and sell this cloth, Granny, and keep the money."

The old woman looked at the cloth and exclaimed, "No, my child! Such cloth is fit only for the king. I will take it to the palace."

The old woman went to the palace and walked back and forth beneath the windows of the king's chambers. The king saw her and asked, "What is it you want, old woman?"

"Your royal majesty," the old woman replied, "I have brought you some wonderful material, and I will show it to no one but you."

The king ordered that the old woman be admitted to his presence, and when he saw the cloth he was astounded.

"How much do you want for it?" he asked.

"It is priceless, your majesty! I have brought it as a gift."

The king thanked the old woman and sent her off with many presents.

The king ordered shirts for himself to be made from the cloth. But no seamstress could be found to do such fine work. Finally the king summoned the old woman and said, "If you were skillful enough to weave this cloth, then you must be skillful enough to make shirts from it."

"It was not I, my lord, who spun it and wove it," said the old woman. "It was the work of my foster daughter."

"Then have her make the shirts!"

The old woman returned home and told Vasilisa what the king had said.

"I knew," said Vasilisa, "that this was something I would have to do myself."

She shut herself in her room and set to work. She sewed without stopping until a dozen shirts were ready.

The old woman took the shirts to the king. Vasilisa washed herself, combed her hair, got dressed and sat at the window, waiting to see what would happen. Soon royal servants appeared in the courtyard. They entered the house and, seeing Vasilisa, proclaimed:

"His royal majesty wishes to see the skillful seamstress who made his shirts and to reward her with his own hands."

Vasilisa was escorted to the king, and when he saw her he fell in love with her at once.

"Vasilisa the Beautiful," he said. "I shall never part from you. You will be my wife."

The king took Vasilisa by her hands, sat her beside him, and they were married on the spot. Not long afterward, Vasilisa's father returned and was happy to learn of her good fortune. He remained in the palace with his daughter, and the old woman too was invited to live there. And as long as she lived, Vasilisa kept the little doll with her always in a pocket of her gown.

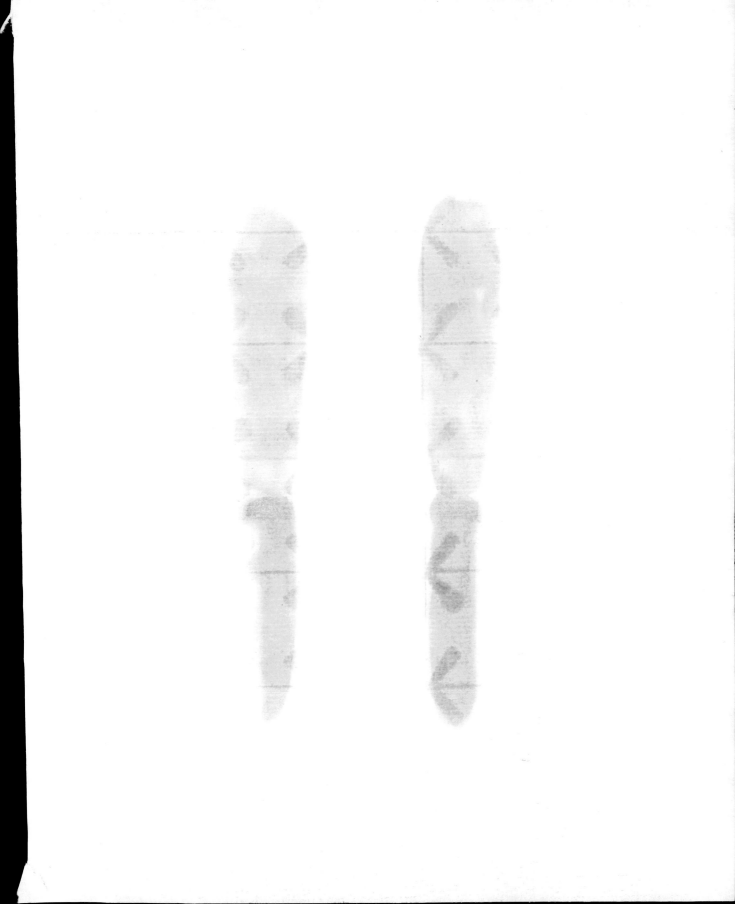